# Jump Ship Jonah

## By Craig Hughes

### Illustrated by Rachel Day Hughes

Clovercroft Publishing

Jump Ship Jonah

©2016 by Craig Hughes

Published by Clovercroft Publishing, Franklin, Tennessee

Published in association with Larry Carpenter of
Christian Book Services, LLC of Franklin, Tennessee

Illustrated by Rachel Day Hughes

Cover and Interior Design by Suzanne Lawing

Printed in the United States of America

978-1-942557-27-2

Dedicated
to my sweet granddaughters,
**EDEN and EMMIE**
who have been the inspiration for this Rhyme Time adventure.


For this book's publication,
many thanks go to
**DEAR FRIENDS**
who have proofread the contents through childlike eyes
and
**HANNAH, CHRISTOPHER and CALEB**
for their unceasing encouragement and timely suggestions along the way
and
**RACHEL**
for her beautifully created artwork of the book's illustrations
and
**KATHA,**
my best friend and wife,
for her constant support and "cheering on" throughout the book's creation.

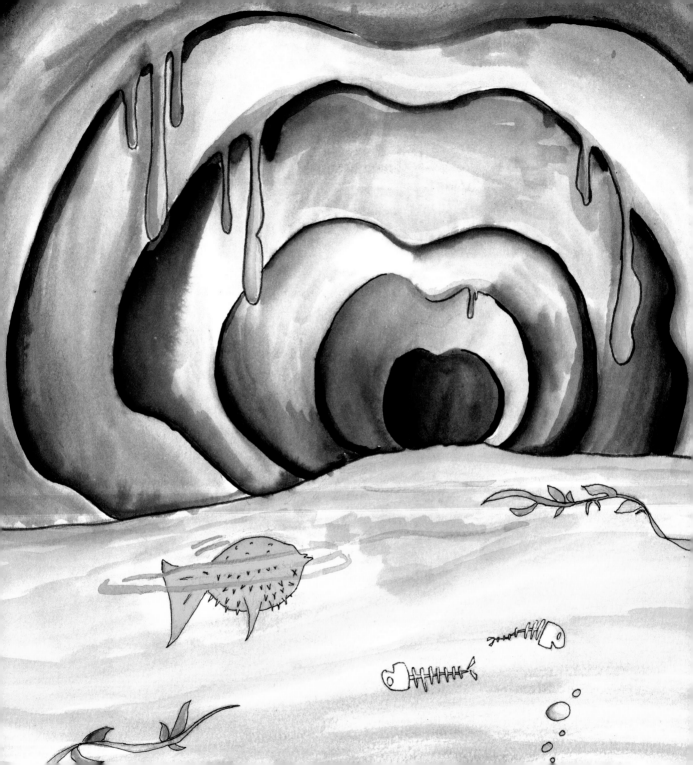

Can you imagine how it feels to be inside a whale,
Surrounded by such slimy stuff and nauseating smell?

Yet that's where Jonah found himself when running from the Lord.
He should have stayed and then obeyed with attitude restored.

It started when Jehovah gave this Jonah special word,
To preach to folk of Nineveh a truth they hadn't heard.

But caring not for Ninevites he formed another plan,
And sailed instead to Tarshish on a ship to foreign land.

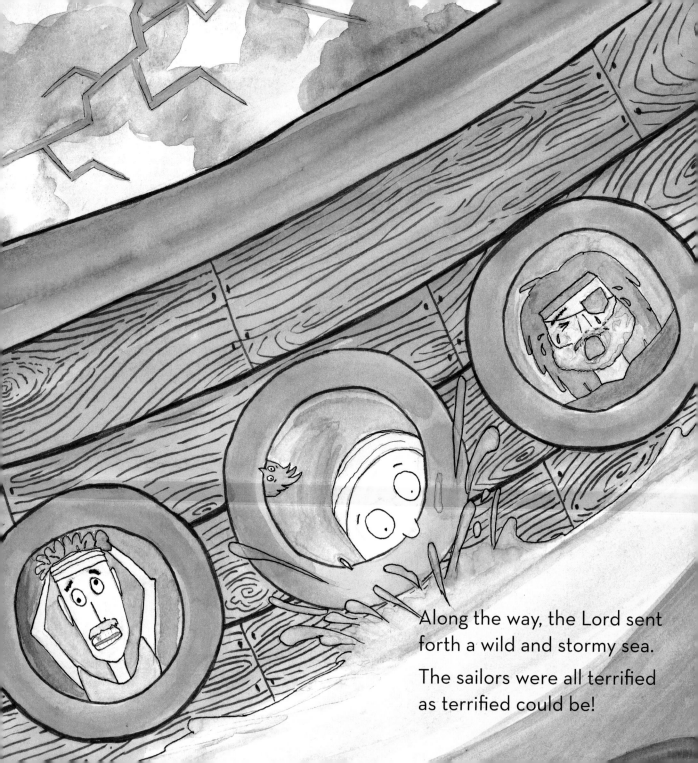

Along the way, the Lord sent forth a wild and stormy sea.

The sailors were all terrified as terrified could be!

When Jonah said he was the cause of such horrific gale,
The sailors threw him overboard, then peace and calm prevailed.

And down, down, down ole Jonah sank to depths of total black,
When God prepared a mighty whale to have a Jonah snack!

Then with a single gulp the whale did swallow Jonah in,
And three long days of solitude in blubber did begin.

When Jonah had a change of heart and he could take no more,
The Lord sent forth the fish to throw him up on local shore.

Then off he went to Nineveh with energy restored,
And started preaching everywhere the warnings of the Lord.

The people took his words to heart, repenting of their ways,
And begged that God would spare their lives throughout the
coming days.

So God in His compassion did not wipe out any thing,
But blessed their true repentance from the pauper to the king.

But this is not the end of Jonah's tale as one might think,
For with a rotten attitude his pride began to stink.

When Jonah saw that God had saved all people of the town,
Instead of great rejoicing, he thought God had let him down.

"I knew that this would happen," Jonah said to God above,
"cause from your great compassion you have chosen to show love.

Instead of bringing swift destruction on this wicked city,
You spared and even blessed them with your mercy and your pity!"

Then storming out of Nineveh, he sat beyond the wall,
To see if God would bring them any punishment at all.

And as he waited angrily to see what might be done,
The Lord produced a vine to shade him from the blazing sun.

The vine made Jonah happy as he napped there with a yawn,
And rested all that day and night until the break of dawn.

Then God sent out a hungry worm to chew the plant away,
Which irritated Jonah as he bore the heat of day.

"What right have you to fume and fuss," said God about the vine.
"Do you care more about yourself than people who are mine?"

The vine is a reminder of God's ever faithful care,
That comes from His compassion even when we say, "Not fair!"

There's much that we can truly learn from Jonah and his story,
But most of all we must obey our God in all His glory.

# LESSONS LEARNED FROM JONAH'S STORY

1. God loves everyone...

     even those who don't love Him back.

2. God wants us to treat others with kindness...

     even when they make us angry.

3. God has a special plan...

     for each person.

4. God can make things happen...

     that might otherwise seem impossible.

5. God can change people's hearts...

     even when we think they won't listen to us.

6. Sometimes life can seem unfair...

     but God is always good.

7. Running away from God...

     always leads to bad things.

8. Helping others...

     makes God happy.

9. Obedience...

     brings blessings.

10. Disobedience...

     brings conflict.